Shaun the She
Takeaway
and
The Farmer's Niece

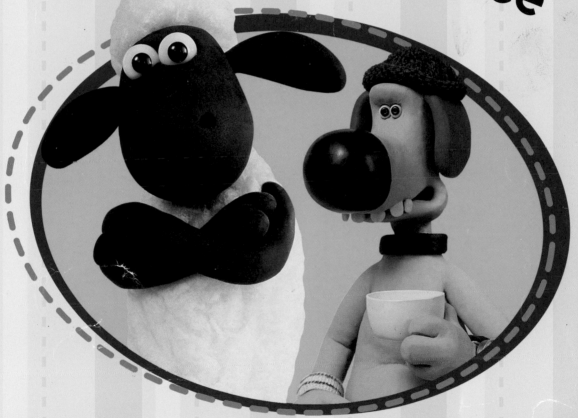

EGMONT
We bring stories to life

First published in Great Britain 2008 by Egmont UK Limited, 239 Kensington High Street, London W8 6SA

© and ™ Aardman Animations Ltd 2008. All rights reserved.
Shaun the Sheep (word mark) and the character 'Shaun the Sheep' © and ™ Aardman Animations Limited.
Based on a character created by Nick Park. Developed by Richard (Golly) Goleszowski with Alison Snowden and David Fine.

ISBN 978 1 4052 3883 0
1 3 5 7 9 10 8 6 4 2
Printed in Singapore

Takeaway

One day, a visitor came to the farm on a loud red scooter. Over in the field, the sheep's ears all pricked up at once.

Bitzer, the sheepdog, woke up from where he was dozing. A scrumptious smell was wafting his way. The flock soon smelled it, too. Together, they flocked to the main gate to investigate.

The Farmer had ordered himself a takeaway pizza. He answered the door and paid the delivery boy. Then, he went back into the farmhouse, without offering Bitzer, Shaun and the flock a single slice.

The Farmer settled down in his armchair and began scoffing down the hot, delicious pizza. He didn't notice the hungry faces of Bitzer and Shaun peering through the window.

The Farmer let out a giant BURP, before falling fast asleep. Moments later, he was snoring loudly.

BURP!

Outside, the sheep's tummies began to rumble . . . almost as loudly as the Farmer's snoring!

Shaun gathered the sheep into a huddle. Why should they settle for grains and grass? They needed a plan, and a cunning one at that.

It didn't take Shaun long to come up with one. He had a baa-rilliant idea — they would dress up as a 'Man' and buy their own pizzas! Shaun signalled with his hoof at the scarecrow behind them.

The sheep sniggered. Shirley, the biggest sheep of the flock, charged at the scarecrow and toppled him to the ground.

Seconds later, he was stripped to his underpants! No coat, no hat, no boots!

Bitzer and Timmy's Mum laid out the scarecrow's coat on the ground. Shaun crawled into the coat first, followed by two more sheep, while another sheep fetched a pair of old leather boots.

Baaa!

Baaa!

Next, Bitzer fetched a long rope to heave the sheep on to their hooves. He looped it through a strong branch, handed Shaun one end of the rope, and the other end to the flock.

Together, the sheep hauled with all their might, and soon the Man was on his feet.

But there was still something very sheepish about their Man. The outfit needed some finishing touches. Timmy trotted over with a pair of old rubber gloves – they would be the Man's hands. Then, Bitzer found some shades. The Man looked seriously cool!

There was just one thing missing — he needed a hat. Another sheep picked up the scarecrow's old hat and was surprised to see a green frog hiding inside. The sheep shook the hat. Hop it, froggie! Then, he tossed it up to Shaun. It was a perfect fit!

The Sheep-Man was ready for action. "Baaa!" cheered the flock.

Ribbit!

PEEP! PEEP!

"PEEP! PEEP!" Bitzer blew on his whistle. The sheep all lined up and Bitzer scribbled down their pizza orders.

With the list of orders safely tucked in his pocket, the Sheep-Man set off. He swayed unsteadily through the main gate and down the country road to wait at the bus stop, with the little green frog hopping behind.

Before long, a double-decker bus pulled up and the Sheep-Man stumbled on board. Luckily, the driver was in too much of a hurry to notice his strange passenger.

The Sheep-Man sat down next to an old lady, who was wearing thick glasses and sucking on a humbug. She offered one to the enormous passenger next to her, but the sheep hadn't practised controlling the Man's rubber hands. The bag tipped over and the sweets inside scattered all over the floor!

The old lady was most annoyed. She grabbed her handbag and whacked the Man hard. The poor sheep were getting a real bruising!

Thwack, thwack, thwack!

Soon, the bus stopped in town. Phew! The sheep were glad to get off the bus and away from the old lady. Now to find the takeaway, thought Shaun.

Shaun passed a map of the town that Bitzer had given him to the sheep at the bottom. The sheep poked his head out of the coat and unfolded the map. The sheep were so busy fumbling with it, they didn't notice a woman walking towards them. She got the biggest fright of her life.

They needed to find the pizza shop . . . and fast!

Aaaahhhhhh!

CLANG!

The sheep dropped the map and wobbled down the street, as fast as their hooves would carry them. Suddenly, Shaun's head bumped into something. CLANG! It was the pizza shop's sign!

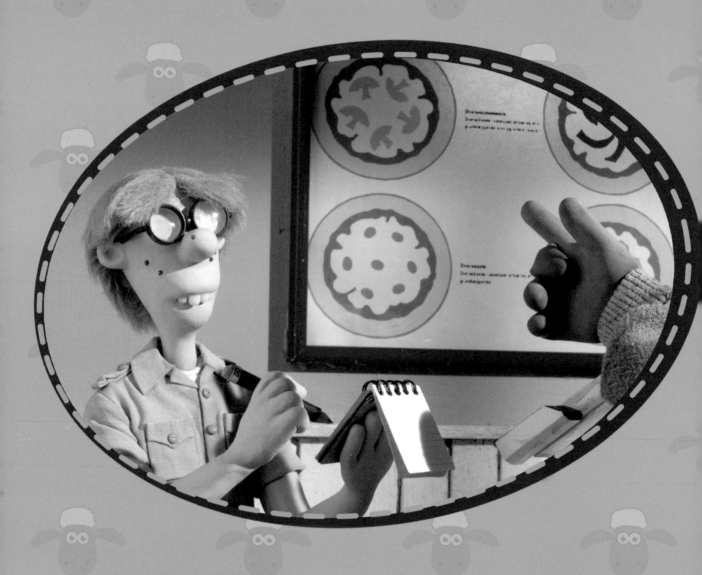

The Sheep-Man swaggered straight inside. There, standing behind the counter, was the same boy they had seen on the farm. "Hmmm?" said the boy, picking up his pencil and notebook to take the order.

Shaun pulled out Bitzer's list and ordered several pizzas by pointing to the menu on the wall.

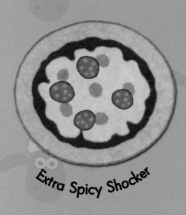
Extra Spicy Shocker

Mighty Mushroom

Porker's Passion

While the pizzas were cooking, the Sheep-Man took a seat. Shaun didn't want to scare any customers that might come in, so he unfolded a copy of the local Ewes-Paper, and hid behind it pretending to read.

Uh-uh!

A little while later, the boy brought out a stack of pizzas. It was almost as tall as the Sheep-Man himself. They smelt scrummy.

The Man reached over to take the pizzas, but a firm hand stopped him. The boy shook his head. He wanted the dough first.

The sheep felt in the coat pockets and pulled out three buttons. "Uh-uh!" frowned the boy.

The sheep felt in the pockets again. Perhaps a comb would do the trick? Nope, that wouldn't do either.

The sheep fumbled through the pockets once more. Suddenly, they felt something slimy. It was the little green frog! It hopped on to the counter. "Ribbit!"

The boy's face broke into a grin. The sheep and the boy had struck a deal – the frog was a fair swap for the pizzas!

Ribbit!

The sheep swiftly picked
up the pizzas, before the boy
could have second thoughts,
and left the shop. Outside,
in an alleyway, they found
a shopping trolley. Perfect!

They loaded it up and set off
home. Though it was getting late,
they didn't want to risk another bus journey.
So they swayed and swerved all the way to the farm.
By the time they arrived, the sun was setting.

Bitzer and the flock had never felt as hungry, so they were delighted to hear the strange trundling of the trolley and its squeaky wheels!

They rushed to the main gate to see the spectacular sight of the Sheep-Man on the horizon, pushing along a gigantic leaning tower of pizzas!

The sheep had waited all day for their pizzas without a bite to eat. They cheered and clapped their hooves as the heroes returned home.

Shaun handed out the pizzas. Each sheep got a whole pizza to himself.

Some sheep were so hungry that they munched down their pizza, box and all! Some had better table manners. Timmy's Mum had swiped a pizza slicer from the trash heap to cut up the pizzas and swap slices.

Little Timmy was looking forward to tucking into his giant pizza. But when he flipped open the pizza box lid, his ears drooped with disappointment at the tiny Timmy-sized pizza.

Baa, baa!

When the feast was finished, the sheep rubbed their bulging bellies happily. Shaun and Bitzer re-dressed the scarecrow as best they could. He looked a bit worse for wear after his trip into town. His clothes hung oddly and his coat was covered in splashes of pizza sauce.

Later that night, the Farmer came out to put his empty pizza box into the recycling bin. Next to the scarecrow lay loads more empty boxes! "Huh?" he muttered. Where could these have come from?

Suddenly, there was a loud BURP! The Farmer looked up to see the scarecrow standing there in the moonlight. It couldn't be, surely? The Farmer wasn't taking any chances, and quickly dashed back inside the house, locking the door behind him!

Shirley baaed from behind the garden wall. She'd gobbled down her pizza so quickly that she'd been burping and hiccupping ever since!

Shaun and the sheep bleated happily – they'd got the better of the Farmer once again!

BURP!

The
Farmer's Niece

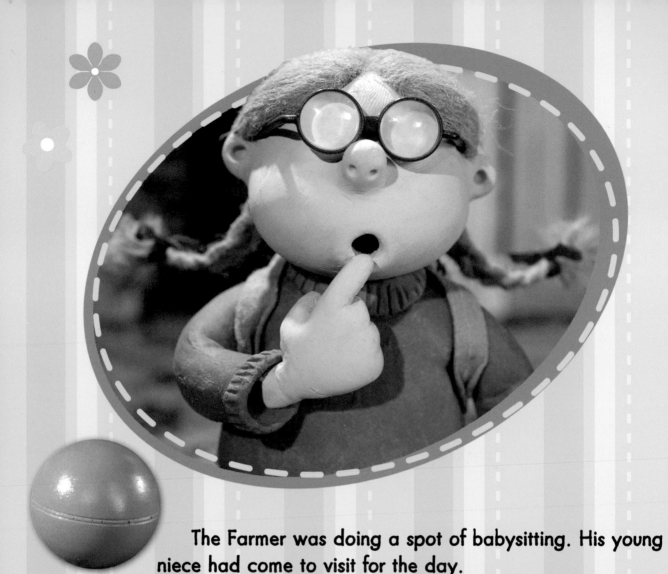

The Farmer was doing a spot of babysitting. His young niece had come to visit for the day.

She'd brought along her favourite pink ball and began bouncing it – indoors. Bounce, boing, bounce!

The girl was clumsy, and the ball soon landed SMACK! on the table. A photo frame flew into the air . . . but the Farmer caught it, just in time!

"Hmmermmm!" he grumbled, pointing OUTSIDE!

The naughty niece smiled back sweetly. She knew he wouldn't stay mad with her for long.

The Farmer was planning to bake a cake as a special treat for his delightful niece . . . the biggest, pinkest, girliest cake ever! But he couldn't keep an eye on her at the same time. So he whistled for his faithful friend.

Bitzer woke with a start from his usual mid-morning doze. "Ruff!" he barked, saluting the Farmer.

Ruff!

Ugh!

The Farmer introduced the pair to each other. Bitzer was to look after her for a few hours. The girl giggled, clutching her pink ball.

"Ugh!" gulped Bitzer. Here comes trouble!

The Farmer went back inside and waved to his niece from the kitchen window. As he busied himself collecting the ingredients for the cake, the naughty girl began to bounce the ball carelessly again.

BOUNCE, BOINK, DONK! The first casualty was a garden gnome, who smashed into pieces.

CRACK!

SMASH!

Bitzer gasped! This girl was trouble with a capital T.

He tried to snatch the ball out of her hands, but she clasped it tightly. Nothing could have prepared Bitzer for what happened next . . .

"WAAH, WAAH, WAAH!" the naughty niece began wailing.

Afraid that the Farmer would scold him, Bitzer let go of the ball and the bawling stopped instantly.

The next moment, the troublemaker was in the sheep's field. Bitzer jumped over the garden wall in hot pursuit.

The Farmer's niece had spied Shaun. She inspected him closely, making baaing and bleating sounds.

BAA!   BAA!   BAA!

The girl noticed another sheep and skipped towards it. Within the blink of an eye she had tied the sheep's ears together in a bow! "Ah!" she cooed, pleased with her handiwork.

"Baaa!" bleated Shaun, shocked. Shaun and Bitzer watched in horror as the naughty niece made her way towards the rest of the flock . . .

Baaa!

Baaa!

Next, she found Timmy, who was pleased to make a new friend . . . until she pulled out his dummy. She thought it was a great game to keep pulling out his dummy and then shoving it back in his mouth, again and again.

Bitzer growled and wagged his finger sternly at the girl. There wasn't going to be any mean business while he was on duty. So he offered to play a game of catch, to keep her out of trouble.

Ruff!

Bitzer was doing a grand job of keeping her quiet until the ball bounced off his nose into the bramble bush behind. Hurrah! smiled Shaun and Bitzer craftily. No more ball = no more playing with the annoying child.

But the naughty niece began to wail again — even louder than before!

Bitzer had to make her stop. There was only one thing for it, he had to get her ball back. Bravely, he made his way deep into the bramble bush. Bitzer was gone a long time. Shaun winced as groaning and moaning noises came from the bramble bush.

Bored of waiting for her ball, the Farmer's niece thought of a new game to play. She pretended she was a sheepdog, and began running around the field yelling, "Ruff, ruff, ruff! Ruff, ruff, ruff!"

That girl is barking mad! thought Shaun. The sheep looked at each other and shrugged their shoulders. Was this a new human game? Because it wasn't very funny. Shaun stood firmly in her way to stop her scaring the sheep.

Then the little girl reached into her pink backpack and pulled out a frilly baby's bonnet. What was she up to now? She put it on Shaun, tied the bow under his chin and shoved a baby's bottle in his mouth . . . all before he could let out a single bleat.

Shaun was not amused. He threw off the baby gear.

Meanwhile, Bitzer had finally stumbled out of the bushes. His fur was covered in thorns and his poor nose looked like a giant pin cushion.

OUCH!

The girl hopped over to play nurse to Bitzer. One by one, she pulled out the thorns. OUCH! Bitzer whimpered woefully.

Then she scrabbled around in her backpack for some bandages. Shaun walked away, shaking his head. By the time she'd finished, poor Bitzer was bandaged up from head to paw!

Before long, the naughty niece had the entire flock wrapped up in bandages, too. Shaun had to think of something to stop this bully in her tracks — and fast.

Suddenly, he spotted a picture of a pony on her backpack. Perfect! He knew exactly how to distract her from teasing the sheep. He would pretend to be a pony! He could do it. After all, he was a sheep of many talents.

Shaun brushed his hooves along the grass, snorting and neighing as best he could. The girl chuckled with excitement.

She quickly exchanged her nurse's hat for a riding cap. The bandages made handy stirrups and reins.

Once on Shaun's back, she commanded the sheep to prepare the field for a One-Time-Only Show-Jumping Spectaculaire.

Bales of hay made excellent seats for the audience. Bitzer and Shirley fetched the drinks. A short-sighted sheep grabbed a pair of binoculars from the scrap heap. Another chose an umbrella (rain was forecast for the afternoon).

The show-jumping course was almost ready. Bitzer, with the aid of the most sensible-looking sheep, took charge of the bar for the jumps.

Round One. The bar was laid flat on the grass. The rider and pony confidently cleared the first hurdle. The crowd cheered and clapped their hooves.

But the little girl wanted more. She ordered the bar to be raised higher . . .

and **higher!**

and **HIGHER!**

Bitzer shrugged and raised the bar a little higher. The unusual rider and pony duo galloped to the start again. "Yeehaa!" called the girl, spurring on her woolly pony.

Shaun cleared the bar again, making it look easy!

"Hee, hee, hee!" giggled the girl. This was a good game.

The audience bleated their appreciation, too. Shaun was simply baa-rilliant!

But the naughty niece was still not satisfied. She wanted to feel like a real champion. She ordered the bar to be raised higher still. It now reached Bitzer's shoulders!

Shaun's eyes narrowed with fear and anticipation. Would he be able to manage it this time? The audience gasped and held their breath . . .

Shaun galloped faster and faster, gaining speed until . . . lift off! He soared through the air, and to the flock's surprise, cleared the bar again!

The crowd went wild. Shaun was a hero!

BAAAAA!

Meanwhile, back in the farmhouse, the Farmer was putting the finishing touches to his cake. He'd made a marzipan pony to sit on the top.

Back outside, his niece was causing a stir. She demanded the bar be moved further back and raised higher. Bitzer and the sheep obeyed – standing on tip-toes, with their front legs reaching for the sky!

The girl grabbed the reins and made her final charge.

Suddenly, Bitzer spotted the Farmer coming out of the farmhouse, carrying the most enormous pink cake he had ever seen! "PEEP!" Bitzer blew loudly on his whistle. He had to warn the others.

He dropped the bar and bounded towards the daring duo. The sound of Bitzer's warning whistle caused a commotion. The sheep began to panic, bleating and baaing for Shaun to stop!

Shaun dug his hooves into the ground and came to a sudden halt, just in time . . .

And now for the show's finale! Shaun stopped in exactly the right spot. The girl flew over the crowd, and landed – SPLAT! – head-first in the cake, splitting it in two!

That's the last we'll be seeing of her, Shaun smirked to himself.

"Grr!" huffed the Farmer. That's it, madam! You're grounded.

He dragged his niece out of the cake and back to the house. No more treats for you, young lady.

Covered in gorgeous, gooey cake, the naughty girl licked her lips and giggled. She didn't seem at all sorry.

As for the other half of the cake, it landed, complete with marzipan pony, slap-bang in front of the flock. "Baaa!" they cheered cheekily, and tucked in!

Woolly Words

Across

1. In Takeaway, the sheep rob him of his jacket, boots and hat!
2. The pizza boy's vehicle.
3. This canine carries a whistle.
4. A female sheep.
5. In The Farmer's Niece, this is on top of the marzipan cake.
6. In the same story, which sheep does the little girl use as a pony?
7. In Takeaway, what does the woman on the bus offer the sheep?

Down

1. Ribbit! This green guy charms the pizza boy!
2. In The Farmer's Niece, the little girl almost breaks it. (Two words, 5 letters each.)
3. In Takeaway, Shaun offers 3 of these to the pizza boy as his first payment.
4. He is the baby of the flock.
5. You can find this in a supermarket. It's handy for carrying lots of pizzas home,too!
6. In The Farmer's Niece, what did the little girl break in the garden?